To
Kenny
Rat Fllomer

W9-CPF-661

# The Boy Who Slept in the Doorway

## Keith Lawrence Roman

Morningside Books

Morningside Books Paperback Edition

Published in the United States of America by
Morningside Books, Orlando, Florida

This edition is cataloged as:
ISBN 978-1-945044-08-3

www.Morningsidebooks.net

Printed in the United States of America

# The Boy Who Slept in the Doorway

# Chapter One

Je m'appelle Doque. My name is Doque. Please try to say my name as something between dough and duck, but call me Duck if it is easier for your tongue.

I am telling you my story so that you may know my life, and that we are completely different, and we are also completely alike.

I am the boy who sleeps in the doorway. I lay all night in the opening of the two doors that open into the rooms of Mademoiselle Jacqueline. My bed is a small grass mat, set upon the soft carpet. I have no blanket for I am not meant to sleep well. I am meant to sleep with both ears and one eye open. Should anyone try to enter the room, my job is to hear, see and call the alarm. This is my job for which I am fed and given clothes.

I am a boy ten years old and I am not yet four feet tall. This last is very important for my bed is only four feet long, and should I grow too tall I will lose my bed and lose my job.

I am not paid for my job. I am given nice clothes and good food. In the summer my food is mangoes, pomelos and cool vegetables. In the winter, I have warm pho soup filled with rice noodles, cabbage, carrots and spicy radishes. I like the radishes best. In the summer, I wear very clean white shorts, a white shirt with a collar and sandals with straps and metal buckles. In winter, I will be given long pants, a sweater and I truly hope, some shoes.

It is not so easy to explain my job. To start, I am a servant in the presidential palace of my country. I live in my city of Hanoi, in my country Viet Nam. My country is very beautiful. It is a land of mountains and jungles and seashore. These mountains have tall forests. The jungles are filled with animals like elephants and monkeys and sometimes dangerous cobras and leopards.

For you to know more of where I am, simply know that the Earth is round and I am away from you, on the other side of it.

Oh, and there are no cobras or leopards in the palace.

The palace sits high on the top of the tallest hill in my city, a hill that flooding water could never climb. The palace is made of stone and cement. There are forty four, twice as tall as I am, glass windows (I know, I counted them). These are actually glass doors. Each of these window doors opens to a small balcony with an iron railing. The roof is made of red clay tiles that never leak water on you while you are sleeping. It rains often here and a roof that never leaks is a wonderful thing. The house has three floors and a basement. There are government offices on the first floor. Mademoiselle Jacqueline who is the daughter of Monsieur Brevie', and her family live on the second floor. Servants live at the very top where rooms are small and the windows are not doors.

The floors of this palace are polished stone the color of pink sand. On this stone are soft wool carpets with pictures in their threads.

Placed on these carpets are dark wooden chairs and sofas with blue silk cushions. The cushions have thread made of gold also stitched into shapes and pictures. I am not allowed to step on the carpet or sit on the cushions. I know how they feel though, as my feet sometimes lose their way. My hands sometimes brush upon the cushions.

Mademoiselle Jacqueline has a huge room for herself. There is a large bed with poles at each corner and light red silk curtains as sides and a roof. Her room has a long wooden desk, at which Mademoiselle takes lessons in reading and writing and many important things. Placed around her table are four chairs with more soft silk cushions.

There is a door inside Mademoiselle's room that opens to another small room. This is called Le Privat. Inside this room are a sink and a toilette. Oh, there is a large white tub that is used to wash the Mademoiselle. This is called "le baignoire". All of the water in this "Salon de bain" comes from turning bright golden handles. After you do this, water pours from the mouth of a small golden fish into the sink and tub.

# Chapter Two

The palace is filled with soldiers and diplomats. Each wears a uniform. Men wearing blue uniforms with red hats are moving everywhere. These are the soldiers. They patrol the streets in open cars and on motorcycles. Here in the palace they stomp their feet announcing their force. I dare not lay down on my bed when they are near, for they will step upon me surely.

Other men wearing white suit jackets and colored ties too tight for their necks are rushing about with bundles of papers. These men are called diplomats. They rush everywhere. Each seems to be very busy and their jobs are thought very important.

All of them answer the commands of Monsieur Brevie'.

I cannot tell you that my job is very important. My family seems to think so.

My mother is proud because I work in the palace and I sometimes bring sweet cakes home for my brothers. I have two of them younger than I am. My father tells me my job is important because I will learn the ways of powerful men.

In the palace, I know I am not important at all.

Men from my country wearing pants and shirts the color of wet grey rocks and men from France wearing blue jackets and red hats are always moving fast about. They often bump me away as they rush. I am almost always unseen. When I am noticed, I am told, "Get back to your station Duck."

My station, say it as this, "stay c own," and you will be speaking the language of France, is the room of Mademoiselle Jacqueline. She is the daughter of the king. No, that is wrong, not the king... something else. Yes, the general. She is the daughter of Monsieur Brevie' and he is the ruler of France. No, I am wrong again. He is the leader of all of France in China. He is the governor general.

Somehow, and I must tell you I don't understand this, my country belongs to France.

France is a much larger country somewhere far away. Men from France are the leaders of my country. If you walk through the market and listen to my father and uncles and all of the men from my country you will always hear them speak of the these "French men" who are the rulers of many countries.

He tells me that men who believe one thing from the mountains in the north and men who believe another from the low rivers in the south of my country both want freedom, to be rid of the French men.

My father tells me that the way things are changing, someday, I may be the ruler of Viet Nam.

Truly though I am mostly hoping for some shoes.

*Keith Lawrence Roman*

# Chapter Three

Mademoiselle Jacqueline is very pretty. She is small as I am, but older by two years. She has dark hair that is not black like mine. It is the color of a deer in autumn. And her eyes also belong to that deer. Mademoiselle Jacqueline has many servants. She has a lady to help her dress, a woman to wash her clothes, she has a woman to teach her reading and writing. She even has a young girl who is made to be her friend.

I am not her friend. I would like to be, but that is not my job. My job is to protect Mademoiselle Jacqueline. I guard her at night. Many people would like to hurt the high governor by hurting his family. These people are angry because the men from France make us work for very little.

They treat us as little more than grains of rice, not the wild rice that grows in the hills, but the plain brown seeds grown everywhere in shallow water across my country.

I am most sad to say that Mademoiselle Jacqueline treats me this same way. I try to understand why this is all so and I don't. I don't understand, but I want to believe that Mademoiselle is quietly kind, that she is only unaware, that she has a good heart inside. Sometimes she says and does things that make me believe this.

One night in late spring, before the heat of summer had settled on the lower land, I lay down on my bed prepared to sleep with one eye always open.

I think I should explain again that my bed is not a bed at all. It is the space on the floor between the hallway and Mademoiselle Jacqueline's room. It is the space where two doors swing open and closed. But they are never closed, for this would block the air. The windows are never open for this would allow danger. So I sleep in my bed, which is not a bed at all, but a space on the floor that any danger would have to step upon.

My job is to lightly sleep with one eye open. And should anything odd wake me, I am to cry out loud.

On that night in spring, the air was cool and wet, as rains had fallen throughout the day. My clothes were still damp from my walk to the palace from our small rice farm. Usually, I am able to beg a little soup or tea from the kitchen. But on this night the kitchen had closed early and the workers had gone home. I shivered as I lay myself down in the doorway on the hard wooden floor. Mademoiselle was being attended to by her governess and teacher, Madame Fornet', preparing for bed by brushing her hair and teeth. I should not have looked in their direction, as Mademoiselle wore only her long nightdress.

"It will be a cool night Jacqueline. Jump into bed and I will find you an extra coverlet" said Madame Fornet'.

She leapt onto her tall fluffy bed and dove under the covers.

"Here you are Jacqueline, this will keep you warm." Madame Fornet' spread an extra, small pink quilted cover over the bed.

Added to the several large feather filled blankets already in place, Mademoiselle would never feel the slightest cold.

"Thank you, Madame," said Jacqueline.

"You're welcome dear. Sleep well." She gave Mademoiselle Jacqueline a soft peck of a kiss on the top of her head and clicked off the small light on a stand by her bed.

The room was not left in darkness, as a small lamp in her bath remained on through the night. The governess moved quietly through an inner doorway to a smaller room where she slept in a smaller, far less opulent, bed.

I lay there on my bed, wanting to sleep, but the wet and cold would not allow it. My teeth clicked together, as my body shivered. I lay on my side and curled myself together, using my arm for a pillow. As each minute of night continued, I felt worse than the minute before.

A tiny shadow drifted across the floor. I lifted my head to look for danger, just as the small pink quilt from Mademoiselle Jacqueline's bed fell across my shoulders.

"Goodnight Doque," I heard softly.

# Chapter Four

I slept soon after and through the night, until dawn passed through the tall windows of Madame Jacqueline's room and woke me. Mademoiselle and Madame were both still asleep. The small blanket still covered me. I quickly and quietly placed it at the foot of Mademoiselle's bed, so that it would appear as if she had kicked it down with her feet. The night had passed and I could leave my station. I rubbed the stiffness from my arms and shoulders, as I walked down the stairs to the kitchen. There I found tea and cakes and a fat sausage one of the soldier guards had neglected to finish eating.

Each day, after I have visited the kitchen of the palace and received a meal, I go home to the house of my mother and father.

My family lives one hour's walk from the deep city where I have my job. The house of my father is much smaller than the house of Monsieur Brevie'. It is smaller than the room where Mademoiselle Jacqueline keeps her bed. It may even be smaller than Le Privat.

My father's house is built of bamboo wood. These thin tube trees grow quickly, so they are plentiful. This wood is tied together to make many parts of a house such as walls, floors and beams for a roof. The house stands on legs cut from palm trees, that keep the house dry above the land. The land is usually dry itself, but when the season of rain comes, water climbs up the legs of the house.

There are no glass windows in this house. When the rains come, we close woven grass doors over the openings in the walls. We then sit in darkness or light a lantern.

Our house has a carpet made from woven mats of grass. Our beds, chairs, tables and almost everything in the house are made from grass and bamboo.

My mother and my father, with my two brothers and my aunt and uncle, work together to plant rice in the fields.

When the seeds are planted, the fields are covered with water. This keeps the plants safe from weeds and insects. When it is time to harvest the rice, we empty the field and walk onto it with sharp sickle knives.

# Chapter Five

My father told me that Mademoiselle Jacqueline's father, Monsieur Brevie' is a good man. He says that we have water for our farm because Monsieur Brevie' ordered the soldiers to dig wells and canals. Before Monsieur Brevie' was the governor, all the soldiers did was march and ask loud questions of anyone in the street.

"Where are you going?" they asked my mother one day, as she was walking home from the market. She answered in our language that she didn't speak French and couldn't understand them.

"I said, where are you going?"

The soldiers are quickly angry. My mother was frightened and tried to simply walk away. But the soldiers blocked her from leaving.

One of them knocked her bags from the market from her hands. She turned to him and said," Tôi chi ve nhà," which means, "I am just going home."

She then scurried to pick up some oranges that were rolling away from her bags on the ground. When she bent over to reach, one of the soldiers pushed her from behind with his foot and her face slid into the ground.

"Arrest her for questioning," one said. And another took a piece of fence wire from a hook on his belt. He wound it around my mother's hands many times until her hands were tightly tied together behind her. My mother cried out as she was dragged backwards by her bound hands through the streets to the jail.

I know this story because my father tells it to me often. He tells me, "This was before Jules Brevie' came to French China. Things were very bad then. It's much better now."

But still my mother refuses to walk to the market alone and has a mark on her cheek from a stone on the ground. When I see the mark on her face, I am angry at everyone.

My father is right though. Monsieur Brevie' is a good and kind man. I know this because he smiles at me when he comes to see his daughter Jacqueline. One time when Mademoiselle was ten and I was eight years old, he walked her to her room from their having dinner together. They stopped at my station, her doorway. I stepped back so that she might enter. Monsieur Brevie' bent down and kissed the top of his daughter's head. To my surprise, he then moved a bit and did the same to me. He said, "doux." This means sweet.

At tables near the market, the men sit and talk with anger. They say the general is coming and he will wash the city in blood from France. I know why they are angry. They too have mothers who have been pushed to the ground, like mine. But still, Monsieur Brevie' has never done this. The soldiers have. But the men say, "Jules Brevie' is the head of a long serpent."

"Father," I say with my eyes lowered, "is Monsieur Brevie a serpent or a man?"

My father smiles at me but then answers in a deep slow tone.

"Doque, Monsieur Brevie' is a man like any other. He answers to law for his crimes and answers to God for his sins."

I think my father is very wise, for a rice farmer.

The French men are all Catholics believing in their God Jesus. My father believes in the words of the prophet Buddha and the words of the prophet Confucius. He also believes in the words of the prophet Jesus. He has told me many times…

"Good men know how to share the heart of God."

So, I know for certain from this that Monsieur Brevie' is a good man and not at all a serpent.

*Keith Lawrence Roman*

# Chapter Six

Madame Fornet' however is definitely part serpent. She makes Mademoiselle Jacqueline sit at her desk for hours reading aloud and writing sums of numbers.

Should I foolishly come by my station an hour or two early she grabs me by the wrist and exclaims, "Doque, you are just in time to join us. Stand at the door and listen."

She catches me like that far too often. Once caught, I stand in my station as Mademoiselle Jacqueline reads over and over from the same books. I have enjoyed her telling of musketeers and princes. But the learning of numbers, added and divided, is a soft torture for me.

"77 divided by 11 Jacqueline?" Madame asks strongly.

"7," Mademoiselle answers.

"99 divided by 9?" She asks.

"9" is heard.

"Wrong, Jacqueline," and then Madame teacher looks at me. But I am not allowed to speak, but I would like to say my guess of 11. Madame Fornet' reads my eyes and nods her head.

"11, Jacqueline. The answer is 11."

And so passes the afternoon with myself a captured counter.

Today, when her teacher came with books and paper, Mademoiselle Jacqueline repeated loud all her lessons in arithmetic. She is learning to use numbers. And I watch and listen. The teacher sits beside Mademoiselle, and I am invisible behind them. She writes 4 times 5 equals 20, 4 times 6 equals 24, 5 times 6 equals 30. And all things are equal until 12 times 12 equals 144. After that, I am lost. Each day more numbers are taught.

Reading and writing in the languages of France and England is also taught. I have learned that in English, "Miss" means Mademoiselle. When speaking in English the teacher is Mrs. Fornet and Mademoiselle is now Miss Jackie.

## The Boy Who Slept in the Doorway

In the language of Viet Nam she is Hoa hau. Say this as, "Hoe How Jack Key."

My father speaks a different language of France called Tay Boi. It is a mix of Viet Nam and France. In the house of the governor, no one may speak this way. My mother speaks very little of any language. But, when she does speak, she uses the language of Viet Nam.

Finally, a tiny clock that Madame Fornet' brought with her and set upon the table rings a bright busy bell. Four o'clock has come. Lessons are over for another day. Madame Fornet' leaves for a while, as Mademoiselle's maid Brigitte arrives. I am excused from my station. With great joy, I walk away, with my walk soon becoming a run. By the time I have reached the stairs for servants at the end of the hall, my feet no longer require the ground. I leap and I fly down steps five and six together. My flight ends at the entrance to the huge warm palace kitchen.

Here I become a small thief. I am allowed meals twice a day, but an occasional cake or bowl of soup disappears each time I arrive.

The cooks do not allow this, but they are always busy preparing special dinners for the men in white jackets with ties and boxes with meals in them for the soldiers guarding the governor's palace. There are 100 boxes for 100 men.

Half of these 100 soldiers are men from my country loyal to France. They stand on the palace balconies with ready rifles in their hands. Thirty more of these Vietnamese soldiers walk the grounds, looking into the bushes with daggers fastened to the ends of their rifles. The last twenty soldiers are from France. They wear blue uniforms and red hats. They wander the halls of the offices on the first floor of the palace. They are there to guard Monsieur Brevie' with their very lives.

One of these French soldiers is my friend. His name is Sergeant Jacques. He is tall and very fat. He has a brush of hair under his nose that is twisted with pointy ends. When I go to the kitchen for one of my extra meals, he whistles a song should anyone be coming to catch me. He taught me this song called Frere Jacque.

## The Boy Who Slept in the Doorway

Frere Jacque
Frere Jacque
Dormez vous?
Dormez vous?

# Chapter Seven

Summer has arrived and even though it rains every day in the afternoon, I am no longer cold at night. Mademoiselle's little blanket is folded and stretched across the foot of her bed. Her feet under her covers do not even touch the edge of it.

After I borrowed a small loaf of bread and some pork noodle soup from the kitchen, I stepped outside to quickly eat this supper. The moon showed only a piece of its circle and the stars were extra bright. The air was clear and the trees were still and silent.

The guards were not near and I wondered if they had found a quiet room to play cards or cast dice in. The palace guards were not the regular French soldiers.

The palace guards were Vietnamese who had adopted the Catholic faith. Most of the soldiers were Catholic. Most of the farmers, like my father are not.

I placed my bowl in a large sink and began to climb the servant's stairway. After climbing four flights of steps, I tread toward Mademoiselle's doorway. The stomping around of soldiers had ended. I thought that they most definitely were playing cards somewhere and drinking wine.

Mademoiselle Jacqueline was seated at her table. Her governess was absent.

When she saw me, Mademoiselle seemed quite pleased.

"Doque, it's good that you are here. I am ready for sleep and there is no one to prepare my bed." I looked at her lost. She read my face completely.

"No, Doque, I don't mean for you to make my bed… just find Madame Fornet' or my girl Brigitte.

"I will go look." I said. I had not noticed before, but now it was clear. The palace was nearly empty.

Monsieur Brevie' had taken Mademoiselle's mother down the hill into the city to see the water puppet theatre. He took most of the upstairs guards with him, as protection.

But where was the governess, Madame Fornet'?

I had not noticed before, but the upstairs was oddly empty. Usually there were 10 or 12 people nearby Mademoiselle Jacqueline's room. The local guard made up from Vietnamese loyal to France alone numbered six to eight. I looked in every open room on the second floor of the palace. All were locked or empty, except that of Madame Brevie's uncle Charles. He lay on his bed asleep with an empty bottle of wine on the stand nearest his bed. He would be slow to wake.

I continued my search down the stairs into the kitchen. It was after dinner hours, but still a cook or a cleaning person should have been there. There was no one. No guards, no maids, no cooks and where was Madame Fornet'? She normally slept in Mademoiselle Jacqueline's room. She sometimes went out in the evening, but never when Monsieur and Madame Brevie' were not in the palace.

## The Boy Who Slept in the Doorway

I took a cake from the empty kitchen and climbed up the rear stairs back to the second floor. By the time I had returned to the room of Mademoiselle, the cake was safely hidden in my stomach.

While I was away, Mademoiselle Jacqueline had dressed herself in her night clothes and was already half asleep in her bed. I was not quite ready to begin my job and so I sat on the floor with my back along the door frame wondering if I should go back to the kitchen for another cake. A yawn from my mouth convinced me to lay down on my side and rest my eyes.

*Keith Lawrence Roman*

# Chapter Eight

Mademoiselle Jacqueline had been asleep for almost an hour when they came. I heard them before I saw them. Their soft canvas and rubber shoes did not make the familiar stomp clomp of the boots on the palace guards. Instead each foot fall landed with a soft flut flut sound. Flut flut, flut flut, someone was running up the stairs. I was still laying down, but was able to look down the hallway to the servant's stairway.

By then there was shouting heard from the floor below. Mademoiselle Jacqueline sat up straight in her bed. The only light was the light from her bath. The hallway was dark. Far at the end of the hall yellow light from two lanterns such as my family used in our farm house appeared.

There were four men, two with the lamps and two with rifles. The rifles had daggers on the end of the barrels. The men holding the lanterns had knives in their other hand.

My station, my bed, the doorway to Mademoiselle Jacqueline's rooms was halfway down the length of the hallway. Monsieur Brevie's rooms were at the far end.

The men with the lanterns were opening every door. If a door was locked, the largest of the men broke the lock and kicked the door open with a crash of his foot. The others then rushed into the room with their rifles and daggers ready.

The rooms upstairs were reserved for the governor general's family and guests. Small rooms were attached to each large one for servants, bathrooms and storage.

In the near darkness, Mademoiselle Jacqueline cried out.

"Madame Fornet' Madame Fornet'." The governess was not there to answer. The men in the hallway had checked four rooms. No one had been in them, except the old uncle of Madame Brevie' who had not wanted to see the shows that night.

From that room came a deep voice of surprise.

"Aidez-moi! Help me! Aidez-moi, someone ple…"

His voice suddenly stopped. The men were moving more quickly now and I could see them in the hall. They wore the dark gray green uniform of a jungle soldier. I had seen these men when my father and I carried rice in a cart we pulled up to the mountains. They were Viet Minh. Soldiers of the old general, fighters for a free Viet Nam.

They wanted freedom from the French. While most of the fighting took place in the mountains, these men had come to the capital city. The Viet Minh hated all the French, especially the head of the serpent. I am sure they had come to kill Monsieur Brevie'. But Monsieur Brevie' was not here. He and Madame Brevie' were enjoying the puppets at the theatre at the bottom of the palace hill. With no Monsieur Brevie' to kill, they would kill or capture anyone they could.

My job is to sleep in the doorway of Mademoiselle Jacqueline, and to cry out if anyone should try to cross into her room.

But who should I cry out to? The local guards had all abandoned the palace. The French guards were with Monsieur Brevie'. Who could I call to? If I cry out now all that will happen is I will be made silent like Madame Brevie's old uncle.

*Keith Lawrence Roman*

# Chapter Nine

"Doque, Doque," Mademoiselle whispered to my shadow laying along the floor.

"Where is Madame Fornet'? What is happening?"

I stood up and went to her bedside.

"Mademoiselle, soldiers from the hills have come to kill. They would kill any French they could. Your parents are not home. Your teacher is away. You must hide right now." I quickly looked around the room for a place that she might hide. The voices of the soldiers were now just two rooms away.

I took her hand and pulled her off the bed. "Lay down in the doorway." I pushed her down to the woven grass mat and moved her legs to block the entrance, just as I slept every night.

With her long pretty hair and satin nightgown, anyone could see she was not a servant.

"This will never work," I said. Then I saw the small blanket folded at the foot of the bed. I pulled it from the bed and covered Mademoiselle just as she had covered me once.

"Now please snore Mademoiselle. Make yourself seem sound asleep. Time was empty as the soldiers were but seven steps away. I leapt onto Mademoiselle Jacqueline's bed and wrapped myself in all her covers.

Mademoiselle had a small night cap under the blankets. I pulled this bonnet over my hair and ears. Most of my face was covered as well. As the men rushed into our room I heard Mademoiselle pretending to snore as loudly as I do. Through a space in the covers, I saw one of the soldiers kick Mademoiselle's covered body. Her body stopped snoring and lay still.

I saw nothing else, as the blankets around me were turned into a fisherman's net and I was swooped up from the bed. Like a sack full of fish, I was carried on the back of one of the men.

As the men stepped over the boy who slept in the doorway, I heard her make a soft moan. Inside the blanket sack, with Mademoiselle's bonnet on my head I smiled and almost laughed.

In Vietnamese, I understood them talking as they ran down the hallway to the stairs.

"The governor general is not here, but we have his daughter and we will send him her fingers, one by one." My captor and I thumped down the stairs and were out of the rear palace kitchen door in just a few small moments.

An alarm had been raised and the shouting voices of French soldiers could be heard.

"Shoot anyone, even the local guard."

The local guard had been warned of the attack and had betrayed Monsieur Brevie'. They had left hours before and were nowhere near the palace. The only men present were the French soldiers and the jungle Viet Minh, and myself, wrapped in a sack made of blankets, being carried away into the night.

The Viet Minh streamed away from the palace through the rear gardens as the French soldiers charged in from the front.

Shots were fired from the soldiers. I don't know if they saw us fleeing or were simply firing into the night, but I felt this was the time for me to try and escape.

I kicked at the back of the Jungle soldier. I kicked as hard as I could at his lower back. He cursed me in Vietnamese.

I would have cursed back at him, but I did not yet want him to know he had the wrong cat in his sack. I stopped kicking just as I was tossed into the back of a small open three wheeled truck. My carrier called to the driver as we sped away through the crowded night streets.

"Take that precious princess to the hills and General Minh. He will know how best to value her life."

I pulled free of the blankets and looked back to see many of the Viet Minh changing their clothes, becoming ordinary people invisible to the French soldiers. They would not need to hide to be hidden.

I cannot tell you exactly what happened in the palace, as I was mistakenly taken away. But, from what I was told, the regular French soldiers quickly recaptured the empty palace.

Monsieur Brevie' led the soldiers as they charged into the Mademoiselle Jacqueline's room. There she was found afraid, silently crying laying under the small quilt exactly where the jungle soldiers had left her.

- Papa des hommes sont venus nous tuer. Ils ont pris Doque.

"Papa, men came to kill us. They took Doque."

Monsieur Brevie' was no doubt confused.

- Ils ont pris Doque?

- Oui, il prétendait être moi.

"They took Doque?"

"Yes, he pretended to be me."

I hope Monsieur Brevie' smiled and thought that all of the cakes I had stolen were worth the value of the Mademoiselle.

The next day Mademoiselle Jacqueline and her mother returned to France forever. Monsieur Brevie' remained.

# Chapter Ten

I was still in the back of the little three wheeled motorcycle truck traveling up small dirt roads to the middle of the mountains. The road was nothing but holes and bumps and I was afraid to come out from under the covers.

We had travelled for what felt like many hours when the warmth of the sun made it impossible for me to stay under the blankets. With the driver looking forward, I looked at the land beside the road. We had crossed some hills and were now riding along a small stream through a long green jungle valley. On one side of the road, fields were flooded for growing rice. On the other, low cinnamon bushes formed a thin wall. The thick leaves of tall Jelutong trees created a canopy from the sun.

The cycle truck had slowed its speed to a little more than a tall man might walk or a ten-year-old boy might run. The driver was bored and singing to himself.

With one quick move I leapt to my feet and jumped off the back of the little truck. I am proud to say that I never even stumbled when my feet landed on the sand of the road. I hopped for 6 steps and darted into the woods. My captor might not have even noticed I had left, except that my jump changed the weight of the cycle truck making his steering jump. He looked back to see the empty cargo space and stopped his truck in seconds.

I could hear him shouting as I ran deeper into the jungle. Mademoiselle Jacqueline's night bonnet was still on my head as I jumped over fallen logs along the path. I pulled it off and let it fall. I then turned away from the path and began to run back toward the road. Through the trees I saw the driver stop to pick up the small bonnet. It was then I understood that he was looking for a small brown haired French girl, not a small black haired Vietnamese boy.

My running took me back to the road 100 meters ahead of the motor tricycle. I walked along the road towards it. The driver had returned to the road and asked me as I walked past him.

"Did you see a young foreign girl anywhere?"

I answered him in Tay Boi the language of common people.

"No Mister, the only one I have seen for an hour is you."

"If you see anyone at all call out," he said.

Noticing the rifle slung on a strap across his back, I was more polite.

"Yes sir, I will look for you as I walk."

"Good," he said, as he went back into the woods to search for Mademoiselle Jacqueline.

# Chapter Eleven

The ride in the back of the motor tricycle had taken two hours before my escape. By the time I reached my parent's home in the city by walking, it was almost dark. My father and mother had the windows shut and a lamp lit over the steps leading from the ground to our house on poles. I was much more tired than I knew for when I was finally home, all I could do was call out.

- Me, cha, con trai cua mình là nhà.
"Mother, Father, your son is home."

My parents and two brothers pushed open the door so fast that one of the straps used as a hinge tore. They jumped down the steps and surrounded me.

They mostly carried me up into the house and in my fatigue, I let them lay me down on my brother's bed, a soft grass mat covered with soft pillows. After bouncing being captured by the soldier, bouncing in the truck and walking so far back to home, my brother's bed felt like a small silk cloud.

Everyone asked me a hundred questions. I remember answering them but I don't remember what I said.

I do remember the next day when my father placed me on the cart we used to carry the rice and proudly wheeled me into town. We must have looked odd to the people of the city as he pulled me through the narrow streets towards the presidential palace. Friends of my family saw us and called out.

"Where are the two of you going?"

"Why is Doque riding?"

We didn't answer anyone. We just quietly rolled on. As we neared the palace, people we didn't know called out.

"If you are going to the palace to work, don't bother. Only French are allowed in the gates. The local guards have been fired or arrested."

We quietly rolled past them up to the gates of the palace wall. French soldiers were standing at the gate with rifles in their hands. Scaffolds had been built behind the wall for more men with rifles to stand upon. At every window and balcony of the palace stood a soldier with a gun. The soldiers at the gate were rude to my father before he even spoke.

"Move your yellow ass away and along or you will be shot." They pointed their rifles directly at us. My father was not afraid. I was afraid enough for both of us.

"Tell Monsieur Brevie' that Doque Thang is here to see him." The soldiers laughed. One fired a shot near to my father's feet. My father jumped and the sound of the gun brought six more soldiers running to the gate. One of them was the sergeant who pretended not to see me take cakes from the kitchen. He pressed past the guards and out to us on the road.

"Doque, Doque you are alive! Taking the handle of our cart from my father he wheeled me through the gate forcing the guards to jump aside.

He was excited calling out to me and anyone who could hear as he wheeled me fast up the palace steps and directly through the grand front doors. My father, with three of the sergeant's men, chased behind us.

"Governor Brevie', Governor Brevie', Viens ici! Viens ici! Come here! Come here!"

The sight of the huge sergeant calling out as he pushed our poor cart through the grand hallway of the palace drew everyone from every room, including Monsieur Brevie' himself.

We all met together in the center of the grand entrance room, The sergeant, his soldiers, my father, Monsieur Brevie' and myself, still sitting in the cart. The sergeant smiled and pointed with two hands at me.

"Voila, our hero," he said.

Monsieur Brevie' came to me and kissed both sides of my face.

"My child, my son, wonderful child." He turned to everyone in the room.

"Here is the one, the only one who did not run away. Here is the one who saved my daughter."

It seemed that everyone was aware of the trick Mademoiselle Jacqueline and I had played on the jungle soldiers. The crowd around us burst into applause.

Monsieur Brevie' lifted me down from the cart and with his hand waved to my father that we should both follow him.

# Chapter Twelve

And so we did. We walked down the long hallway towards Monsieur Brevie's office. The sergeant followed, not one step behind us, unwilling to leave our side.

"Doque please sit," He offered my father his hand. "Excuse me, I don't know your name." My father answered in French.

"Je m'appelle Tuan Thang."

Monsieur Brevie' gestured with his hand and spoke. "Please sit both of you."

"Is Mademoiselle Jacqueline safe and well?" I asked.

Brevie' was pleased as he answered.

"She is fine Doque. She and her mother are on an aeroplane back to our home in Paris. She has ordered me to find you, thank you and say that you are her true brave friend.

"She said to tell you she is proud of you and that I must never let you sleep without a blanket on a cold night." Monsieur Brevie' laughed as he said that last part.

'Truly, young man, we had great doubts that you were still alive." He turned to my father. "Many from both sides died last night." My father nodded wisely. "My wife's uncle and my daughter's teacher were among those lost." They were surprised by the Viet Minh, she in the garden, he in his room. He looked sad for a moment then returned his eyes to me while still speaking to my father.

"But our two joys were kept by God through the night. Your brave son, our brave son," he said proudly, "put my daughter's life before his own. For this I am forever in his debt." Again he spoke directly to my father.

"Monsieur Thang, we, the French are on the verge of losing a great battle 1000 miles away. France cannot much longer control Indochina. My government will soon leave, and your country will be divided between the old Emperor and the new regime of Ho Chi Minh."

"This I know," said my father.

"Last night your son saved my daughter. But now here is no safe place for him. Within two months, the Communist General Ho will sit at my desk. I will be with my family in Paris. Where will you be? Where can you be? The Viet Minh will not see your son as brave. They will see him as an enemy."

My father nodded his agreement.

"Should we leave our land and move away?" my father asked.

"There will be no land to own when the general comes," said Monsieur Brevie' and he continued. "The big sergeant outside, Jacques, let him take you and any of your family south. You must leave today, for as we speak we are heard. The friends of the men who attacked last night will seek favor with General Ho before he arrives. I am sorry that you must leave but I do not regret my family's safety. All I can offer is my gratitude and passage to a new beginning.

"Sergeant Jacques has a truck with men to drive you. I will give you money for your new life, in what will be a new country, a new state of Vietnam."

He stood up and my father bowed. Monsieur Brevie' stepped over to me and bending over once again kissed the top of my head.

He turned his back to me and his arm reached up to his eyes. He waved goodbye from this stance.

"Go now, both of you and be safe always."
"Sergeant, he called out, "you have your orders. Take care of my new son."

"Mais oui, of course, Monsieur Brevie'" replied the sergeant.

A few more words were spoken, but they did not matter. We left with the sergeant and three of his men. We all rode in the front of a large truck to my parent's farm. My mother and brothers quickly understood that our home would no longer be safe. The soldiers and my father's brother's family helped us quickly put all our belongings in the back of the large truck. My uncle and his family decided to remain but promised us that they would head south and find us, if any danger came.

*Keith Lawrence Roman*

# Chapter Thirteen

We rode for three days in the truck. The land changed greatly as we headed further south. We crossed a line that I could not see. The sergeant called it a parallel. After that, we crossed a river which was easier to see and meant that we were no longer in North Vietnam. We were in South Vietnam and the two looked completely the same.

For one more day we drove south, until the even the smallest of hills did not exist. The air was heavy with heat and mosquitoes. The road was a long thin bridge made of sand, through 100 kilometers of low water. And in that water, were flooded farms of rice. It was at one of these farms we stopped.

With money my parents had saved and money from Monsieur Brevie' we bought another farm with another bamboo house sitting on posts made from palms.

After a month, I realized, nothing too much had changed, except I no longer had my job eating cakes and sleeping in the doorway. I don't think this mattered, as I had started growing taller.

In this Vietnam, I would go to school and find that all of the arithmetic Madame Fornet' had made me hear was quite helpful. I spoke English, French and Vietnamese and worked as a translator for American soldiers who had come to my country after the French had left.

I went to college, married a girl I met at the university and when soldiers from the north took over South Vietnam and made the Americans leave, I left with my wife and children by helicopter and a crowded boat. The boat took us to America.

In America, each of my children has a bedroom almost as fine as Mademoiselle Jacqueline's. And, when I pass through their doorways to wish them goodnight and good dreams, my eyes cannot help but look down.